THE HAPPY LION

THE

By Louise Fatio

Dragonfly Books —————⊰ New York

HAPPY LION

Pictures by Roger Duvoisin

Copyright © 1954, copyright renewed 1982 by Louise Fatio Duvoisin

All rights reserved. Published in the United States by Dragonfly Books,
an imprint of Random House Children's Books,
a division of Random House LLC, a Penguin Random House Company, New York.
Originally published in hardcover in the United States by McGraw-Hill, New York, in 1954.
Dragonfly Books with the colophon is a registered trademark of Random House LLC.
Visit us on the Web! randomhouse.com/kids
Educators and librarians, for a variety of teaching tools, visit us at RHTeachersLibrarians.com

The Library of Congress has cataloged the hardcover edition of this work as follows:
Fatio, Louise.
The happy lion / by Louise Fatio; pictures by Roger Duvoisin.
p.   cm.
"A Borzoi Book"
Summary: When the door to his house at the zoo is left open, a lion decides to visit his friends, but he quickly learns
that people are not nearly as polite or friendly in town as when they visit him at the zoo.

ISBN 978-0-375-82759-4 (trade) — ISBN 978-0-375-92759-1 (lib. bdg.) — ISBN 978-0-553-11364-8 (pbk.)
1. Lions—Juvenile fiction. [1. Lions—Fiction. 2. Friendship—Fiction.] I. Duvoisin, Roger, ill. II. Title.
PZ10.3.F35 Hap 2004 [E]—dc21 2003004194
ISBN 978-0-553-50850-5 (pbk.)

MANUFACTURED IN CHINA
10 9 8 7 6 5 4 3 2 1
Random House Children's Books supports the First Amendment and celebrates the right to read.

There was once a very happy lion.

His home was not the hot and dangerous plains of Africa,
where hunters lie in wait with their guns.
It was a lovely French town with brown-tile roofs and gray shutters.
The happy lion had a house in the town zoo, all for himself,
with a large rock garden surrounded by a moat,
in the middle of a park with flower beds and a bandstand.

SINGES

Early every morning,
François, the keeper's son, stopped on his way to school to say,
"*Bonjour*, Happy Lion."

Afternoons,
Monsieur Dupont, the schoolmaster, stopped on his way home to say,
"*Bonjour,* Happy Lion."

Evenings,
Madame Pinson, who knitted all day on the bench by the bandstand,
never left without saying, "*Au revoir,* Happy Lion."

On summer Sundays,
the town band filed into the bandstand to play waltzes and polkas.
And the happy lion closed his eyes to listen. He loved music.
Everyone was his friend and came to say, *"Bonjour"*
and offer meat and other tidbits.

He *was* a happy lion.

One morning,
the happy lion found that his keeper
had forgotten to close the door of his house.
"Hmm," he said, "I don't like that. Anyone may walk in."
"Oh well," he added on second thought,
"maybe I will walk out myself and see my friends in town.
It will be nice to return their visits."

So the happy lion walked out into the park
and said, "*Bonjour*, my friends" to the busy sparrows.
"*Bonjour*, Happy Lion," answered the busy sparrows.
And he said, "*Bonjour*, my friend" to the quick red squirrel,
who sat on his tail and bit into a walnut.
"*Bonjour*, Happy Lion," said the red squirrel, hardly looking up.

Then the happy lion went into the cobblestone street,
where he met Monsieur Dupont just around the corner.
"Bonjour," he said, nodding in his polite lion way.
"Hooooooooohhh . . . ," answered Monsieur Dupont,
and fainted onto the sidewalk.
"What a silly way to say *bonjour*," said the happy lion,
and he padded along on his big, soft paws.

"*Bonjour*, Mesdames," the happy lion said farther down the street when he saw three ladies he had known at the zoo.
"Huuuuuuuuuuuuuuhhhhh . . . ," cried the three ladies, and ran away as if an ogre were after them.
"I can't think," said the happy lion, "what makes them do that. They are always so polite at the zoo."

"*Bonjour,* Madame." The happy lion nodded again
when he caught up with Madame Pinson near the grocery store.
"Ooh la la . . . !" cried Madame Pinson,

and threw her shopping bag full of vegetables into the lion's face.

"A-a-a-a-choooooo," sneezed the lion.

"People in this town are foolish, as I begin to see."

Now the lion
began to hear the joyous sounds of a military march.
He turned the next corner,
and there was the town band, marching down the street
between two lines of people.
Ratatatum ratatata boom boom.

Before the lion could even nod and say, *"Bonjour,"*
the music became screams and yells.
What a hubbub!
Musicians and spectators tumbled into one another
in their flight toward doorways and sidewalk cafés.
Soon the street was empty and silent.

The lion sat down and meditated.
"I suppose," he said, "this must be the way people behave
when they are not at the zoo."
Then he got up

and went on with his stroll in search of a friend
who would not faint, or scream, or run away.
But the only people he saw were pointing at him excitedly
from the highest windows and balconies.

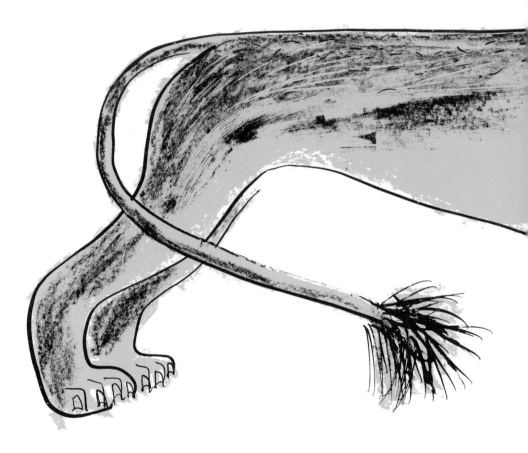

Now what was this new noise the lion heard?
Toootooooot . . . hoootooooootooooot . . . , went that noise.
Hooooot tooooooTOOOOOOOOOHHHOOOOT . . . And it grew

more and more noisy.
"It may be the wind," said the lion.
"Unless it is the monkeys from the zoo,
all of them taking a stroll."

All of a sudden,
a big red fire engine burst out of a side street
and came to a stop not too, too far from the lion.
Then a big van came backing up on the other side of him
with its back door wide open.

The lion just sat down very quietly, for he did not want to miss
what was going to happen.

The firemen got off the fire engine
and advanced very, very slowly toward the lion,

pulling their big fire hose along,

Very slowly they came
closer . . .
and closer . . .
and the fire hose crawled on like a long snake, longer and longer . . .

SUDDENLY,
behind the lion,

a little voice cried, *"Bonjour, Happy Lion."*
It was François, the keeper's son, on his way home from school!
He had seen the lion and had come running to him.
The happy lion was so VERY HAPPY
to meet a friend who did not run and who said, *"Bonjour"*
that he forgot all about the firemen.

And he never found out what they were going to do, because
François put his hand on the lion's great mane and said,
"Let's walk back to the park together."
"Yes, let's," purred the happy lion.

So François and the happy lion walked back to the zoo.
The firemen followed behind in the fire engine,

and the people on the balconies and in the high windows
shouted at last, "*BONJOUR*, HAPPY LION!"

From then on
the happy lion got the best tidbits the town saved for him.
But if you opened his door,
he would not wish to go out visiting again.
He was happier to sit in his rock garden,
while on the other side of the moat
Monsieur Dupont, Madame Pinson,
and all his old friends came again
like polite and sensible people
to say, *"Bonjour,* Happy Lion."
But he was happiest
when he saw François walk through the park
every afternoon on his way home from school.
Then he swished his tail for joy,
for François remained always his dearest friend.